She Forgot To Love Herself

-Through the Eyes of a Best Friend-

Latasha Morrow

Liberation's Publishing LLC
West Point, Mississippi
www.liberationspublishing.com

This is a story of love gain, lost, and found. It is the story of a girl who has been tossed and turned by the winds of love. There is the love we need from our family and the love we need from a lover. Some times we sacrifice one for the other. Kelly's story is just that. Sit back and enjoy as I tell through my eyes her ups and downs on her journey to true love.

-Latasha Morrow

Latasha Morrow

Acknowledgements

My mother name is Margaret Collins and my father name Wendoyln Collins. I have two brothers, Wendoyln Collins Jr and Travis Hammond and two sisters, Tiffany Collins and Courtney Hammond. I will like to also acknowledge my honorary father that have been by my side since birth which is Bobby Nash I really appreciate everything you have done for me as a father figure. Along this journey In life I must admit it was challenging for me due to the fact I used to tease my faith.

After I learned how to give my worries and problem to God and leave them with him I been seeing better things happened for me. I tell you I love my family and friends they mean the world to me. So I will like to give special Thanks to Lekesia Gates, Marlisia Pierce, Lashondra Ivy, Ebony Logan, Yolanda Wofford, Larikka Stevenson, Shawntea Cockrell, Corey and Lajoyce Key These people is literally one phone call away every time I need them.

My Grandaddy Cleotis Randle is my everything, this man doesn't even know how to say NO to me, he's always there when I need him and for that I Love him so much. Estella Ivy I thank you so much for your listening ears, your encouragement words and your warm heart you are like a mother to me. My mother in law Brenda Morrow I Love you so much. Of course I didn't name a lot of people but just know I Love you all! Thank you William and Margaret for being my rock since day one both of you means the world to me.

Table of Content

1 Defining Kelly

As children growing up we all have these big dreams of what we want to accomplish when we grow up. We create a do and don't list for our lives and really believe it will go just that smoothly. Some of us grew up in a loveable atmosphere that allowed us to become the best we can be, while others grew up in the opposite. We never learn self-love, respect, or potential. This is the life for Kelly.

Kelly was a beautiful dark brown skinned woman with a doll face and long shoulder blade length coal black hair. She had a body to die for, flat stomach, tones thighs, and spotless smooth skin. To top it off she had a heart of gold and would go out of her way to help most people. The only problem is she didn't know inside just how beautiful she was. She was a good girl raised in church by her mother, who happened to be one of the best mothers in the neighborhoods.

Kelly's mom and dad made sure she and her sister Monica grew up in the house of the Lord. Faith came first in her life. Her father was a great teacher of the word, and she would often go to him when there were scriptures she didn't understand. Kelly's mom had unshakeable faith, she was hardly ever down. She prayed in all things, and taught them to not hold grudges, kill people with kindness, and they talked about Jesus, and we are no better. Mom was Queen in Kelly's eyes.

Kelly saw her mom go without just so her children could have. She was always praying for their success. So when Kelly didn't finish college it disappointed her, but she prayed for Kelly then too. Procrastination was a big hindrance for her. Life was comfortable she had a nice car, she made good money as a Licensed Practical nurse, and a good man.

Monica was very quiet, hardworking and only entertained her own business. She was about that money and her success. She graduated with a degree in fashion design, and moved away to Atlanta, Georgia. She owns two businesses, a clothing store and a winery. She and Kelly stayed in touch on the regular, texting, emailing, or chatting it up on the phone. Monica couldn't come home much, but she always sent money home to her parents. When Kelly had children she sent money home to them too.

Kelly had these cousins that she loved, and with her sister gone she wanted to spend time with them more than ever. They were trifling though, the frenemy type. Somehow it hadn't sunken in to Kelly yet, She would let their pettiness slide way too often.

You know the type of people that were always saying how other people were pretty or had long hair, but never compliment you. They did this to Kelly all the time. It bothered her so much she cut all her hair off. Keep in mind her hair was to her shoulder blades, and she cut it off up to her ears. It was a bad ass A-line bob pretty and thick, and she was rocking the hell out of it. When they saw it they only found something else to make her feel self-conscious about.

"You're so easy to persuade, Kelly." Her mom would always say. Her mom was always trying to keep them prepared for the world. And don't get me started on the dark joke. Those cousins were always on Kelly about the sun baking her skin. They were all light skinned, Asia being the lightest. Kelly was used to the jokes, and her mom instilled in her head that black was beautiful. She and Monica were both pretty dark-skinned girls with hearts of gold. There mom did not like anyone running over them. Their mom was very over protective.

Monica didn't have a big problem with the cousins. She didn't hang with them and advised Kelly to do the same. "They don't mean you no good." She was always saying. Kelly had to learn the hard way. Like the time Kelly was dating this guy on the basketball team in high school, Kelly was really into him. Come to find out Asia slept with him. Kelly found out about it, and Asia apologized. She said he took advantage of her, because she had been drinking. Since

Kelly was a family person she broke up with him and kept Asia as her favorite cousin.

Kayla, Simone, Asia, and Shayla gave Kelly the hardest time on into her adult life. There was this dinner party they all went to. They're all dressed and ready to go, and Kelly as always is killing it, dressed to the nine. She had on a sexy red dress and some super high heels. Instead of giving her props they just snubbed their noses and asked her why was she so dressed up. What did Kelly do? She went inside and changed. She came back out with a shirt and heels to blend in with them.

They smiled liked chess cats. "That's better." Shayla said being messy. "Ain't nobody going to out dress me." To Shayla's surprised Kelly drew more attention in those jeans than any of her cousins. You know they were rolling eyes and talking about, "That bitch think she the shit." Kelly walked right in on them talking, but she waved it off and carried on the night with them.

Kelly was always getting men's attention, but she had a man and she was very faithful. She was shutting them down left and right, and this gave her hating cousins even more to be jealous of. Simone started this stupid game. It was a bet.

"Kelly I bet you'd never date a thug."

"No, I wouldn't, but when I was younger I wanted to, not now though."

"Why not? You think you better than everybody else?"

"No I just don't think me dating a thug is a good match."

Asia looked at the girls, "Well damn she think she too good."

Kelly started to get upset, "Why ya'll coming at me about men, when you know I got a good man. What's really going on? Why ya'll always saying I think I'm better than you?"

The cousins looked stunned. "Problem." They all said in unison.

"Yeah problem. Ya'll always acting like you have a problem with me."

Not wanting things to get real the cousins all laughed it off. "Girl you over thinking." Said Kayla. We don't have a problem with you girl." That wasn't good enough for Asia. She was determined to push the issue.

"I don't' think you look down on us, but you do look down on other men, especially thugs."

"I do not! I've got a man. Why don't you get that?"

The conversation went back and forth. "There's no sin to mingle with other guys, Kelly. You're not married." Asia insisted. "You may never know what you're missing."

Kelly was in her feeling again. She really wanted her cousins to see her in a different light. "Alright, Alright, I'll step out of the box." This brought on all the cheers. They toasted their glasses and seem to accept her as equal.

2 How to Lose a Good Man

Kelly was really set on taking a chance on a thug. She started acting different with her man. He noticed it but kept quiet. Kelly's cousins started inviting her out with them more, and she was loving that.

The more she would hang out with them the more she would change. She notices that her relationship was falling apart, and she didn't want that to happen. She went and talked to her mother trying to see how she can save her relationship and keep a good relationship with her cousins. Her mother told her "Baby don't be no fool and let that good man go because of your cousins. If they had a good man they wouldn't let you ruin it for them."

Kelly mother reminded her, "if they can't respect your relationship then they don't respect you. It's not your fault that you want and got a good man." Kelly knew her mother would give her honest opinion and she held on to what her mother told her.

She continue to hang with her cousin, because she was having fun with them. One night when they were all out she told the girls that she was really enjoying them, but it was putting a strain on her relationship at home. The girls told Kelly cuz we enjoy you as well, and a song came on and they grab Kelly and went to the dance floor to throw Kelly off the conversation.

They was drinking they ass off. Kelly

didn't usually drink, but she had started drinking just to fit in. She had two mixed drinks and a shot that night and went home. She was drunk.

After getting home and falling asleep on the couch her boyfriend, Bryce came in and just stood there shaking his head at her. He left her on the couch. The next day she had a hangover. She went to visit her mom for a couple of hours. When she got back Bryce had already pack all of her clothes. She was in shock. He asked her to come to the kitchen table so they could talk. She went on in there with tears in her eyes. She already knew that she had mess up.

Bryce looking in Kelly eyes seeing that her eyes was full of tears grabbed her hands and pulled them close. "You know I love you.

"Yea babe, I know."

"You are the most beautiful and intelligent woman I know. This person that you are becoming is not the Kelly I know."

"I know, I know, but I can change."

"Kelly, you've been saying that, but your actions show differently."

"All my life I seemed to have this missing piece."

"What piece is that?"

"Bryce, baby, you know how I love to make everyone happy. I really wanted the bond between my cousins to get strong. I finally have that. I finally have them back in my life, and you want to walk out of it."

"Your cousins don't have your best interest at heart, Kelly."

"Why would you say that!"

"Every since I've know those girls they've always treated you bad. They talk down to you and better yet, they never tried to build a bond with you!"

"Why would you say that? That is not a fair statement! You just want to control my life like everyone else."

"I'm not! I'm not Kelly. I'm not trying to control who you hang with. This new bond you have with those girls is destroying us. You stay out all night. You're drinking way more than usual. It's like you're trying to make me leave."

"Trying to make you leave!" Kelly yells and sobs hysterically. She places her hand on her forehead and talks as if no one is there. "I can't believe this is happening. I can't believe this is happening." She new she was trying to make Bryce leave, but now that it is actually happening she can't handle the pain. "What was I thinking she thought to herself."

Bryce gave her time to calm down, but he wasn't' changing his mind. She did this, Kelly destroyed us. "Babe I love you, but I'm leaving. I wish you the best. I've made sure to pack all your things. I can help you take them home if you'd like."

Kelly continued to be in unbelief. She did let Bryce put her things in her car, but after that she refused to look back and left.

3 Finding a New Man

Kelly called her cousins and told them about what happened. They came over her mother's house to chill with her for a couple of hours. All the while she was sobbing to them they were trying to hook her up with another man.

Kelly's mom was eavesdropping on their conversation, and when she saw that they had no concerns about how Kelly was feeling she ask Kelly to come help her with something. The girls got the point and told Kelly that they will catch up with her later on. Kelly walked them to the door. She looked out the window until they drove off. Then she went to help her mother.

"Ma, why'd you do that?"

"Kelly those cousins of yours mean you no good. They could careless what you just got yourself into, or should I say what you got out of. Bryce was a good man."

"They do love ma. Why do you always have something negative to say about them. They have been spending a lot of time with me. It's been fun. I think you just hate them because they are daddy's nieces." Kelly walked away as her mom stood there in unbelief.

"That child," her mom thought to herself.

Kelly really believed it was about the girls being her daddy's nieces. He mom didn't deal with his folks. Snakes in the grass she always called them.

For an entire month Kelly mourned her dead relationship with Bryce. She'd call her cousins just to talk to them about what she was feeling. They pretended to care, but always got off the phone quickly. She felt worthless, and the only thing that kept coming to her mind was how she let her cousins take her to this place. She had done everything she could to please them and gain their acceptance. "Maybe ma's right." Kelly started hanging with her mom more, and she started to heal.

Kelly's mom went into town every Saturday and on Wednesday and Sunday she went to church. That fall Kelly went back to college, but decided to commute. She was determined to get the LPN program. Kelly was healing, but it still hurt and she missed Bryce terribly. Even though she thought about it she never went to see him and try to make it better.

On campus she met Jacob. He was fine and she fell for him instantly. He also helped fill the void left by Bryce's leaving. Jacob was a good man. He was good to her, but just wanted too much sex. In fact, they had so much sex that over the course of two years she had two babies, twins.

After the twins, she wasn't really able to keep up with Jacob's sexual needs; he started stepping out. Second hole in her heart. She couldn't win for loosing. Jacob let Kelly leave him, but he never stopping loving and taking care of his kids. He was a good father.

4 When Kelly Met Gutta

When Kelly got pregnant her cousins started coming back around again. They were glad to see her down, but didn't show it. It made them feel like they were on the same level in some way. When she broke up with Jacob they were even happier. Kelly wasn't ignorant to there ways now, it just made her happy to have someone to talk to besides her mom.

Kelly had changed a lot after having the babies, she and Jacob had started going to church, and once he left Kelly continued to go and take the kids.

Church helped her keep her sanity, and it gave her peace of mind. In heart Kelly was a good girl. She loved church, singing and praising. She was beautiful, and even though she wasn't seeking attention it always sought her out. She was lonely and desired to be with someone.

Kelly's main focus was her twins. She knew she wanted the best for them. She wanted to find the right man, and whenever she went out on a date she gave deep consideration before saying yes. Kelly's mom was happy with her being single for a while, but once Kelly got bored and horny she knew she had to get back into the dating seen.

Here comes guy number three. He was gorgeous, in church, and knew how to treat a woman. He was charming and had good money that he did not mind spending. Kelly wondered, "why is he not married?" The first time they made love she knew why. This man humped her two hours. How she endured it she had no idea. Now it was good, really good, but by hour two her stuff couldn't take no more. It was swollen and took three days before she could make love to him again.

Kelly's mom liked Mr. Take Too Long Stroking. He wasn't who she wanted Kelly to be with, but Bryce had moved on and gotten married. Kelly's mom did like him though, he had money and was always shower Kelly and the twins with gifts and extra cash. Daddy Long Strokes turned out to not be too happy with Kelly sanctioning his loving. That relationship ended too.

She had been broken up with Daddy Long Strokes for a few months now, and she was getting lonely. Kelly went to the mall to get the twins shoes. While in the shoe store she was startled by a group of guys that walked in laughing and talking. One in particular caught her eye. It was something about him. He had swag and that rough boy appearance. He had pretty teeth that he kept flashing Kelly's way. He wasn't cute, like the guys she had dated before, but it was something about his atmosphere that kept calling her to notice him.

"Hi." He says as he walks by slightly brushing up against her. "Who you shopping for, your nigga?"

"No I'm not shopping for my nigga. Why are you so nosey. You don't know me."

"But I wanna know you, and they way you checking me out you wanna know me too."

"Boy please." Kelly said smiling and feeling all warm inside. He was really getting next to her. She hid it well though.

"A boy I'm not. Gimme your number, so I can take you out and show you."

"I won't."

"Alright then." He snatched her receipt and wrote down his number, as he watched her smile. He signed his name Young Gutta. "Use it." He flirted as he handed the receipt back to her.

"Like I said, Boy Please." She sassed as she walked away switching.

5 Loving Gutta

Kelly refused to call Young Gutta. She wanted to though. It was something about his being that made her think about him all the time. He was sexy to her somehow. After a month had passed she found herself in the mall again. Young Gutta was there of course, "This nigga must live at the mall." She thought to herself. Inside she was hoping he was. He noticed her right away.

"Hey girl, I've been waiting for your phone call." He says as he walks towards her.

"I thought you were kidding."

"I don't play games girl." He said with that sexy voice and flashing those beautiful white teeth. He had a way of looking at a girl straight in the eyes and capturing her like a hypnotist. "Let me see your phone." He says while gently grabbing Kelly's hand and removing it. He dialed his number. "Now you have no excuse not to call me. Better yet, I'll be calling you."

Call her he did. He called her everyday for two weeks. Kelly never answered. This was a new kind of feeling. She was actually drawn to Young Gutta. She was drawn to him in a way that she wasn't sure she wanted to be. Yet and still the last time she answered his phone call.

There was something about Young Gutta, and it wasn't his looks. He had a charm that was enchanting. They talked for hours on the phone. She grew to like him more and more.

Young Gutta was a thug, and that became more and more apparent as she talked to him. Most people in his town were scared of him. His spot at the mall was were he and his crew brought in the most cash. He sold pills to the rich kids at the mall and weed in the hood. They were the type of crew no one wanted to be on their bad side.

This didn't deter Kelly, instead she fell for him hard. The first time they made love was the biggest mistake of her life. It was just like she always wanted it to be. He was a great lover. This made her fall hard for him even more. The fact that this thug could treat her so gently and stroke her so soft was unbelievable. She was hooked. They fell in love hard. He was glad to have a good girl, and dared anyone or anything to come between what he had gained.

Kelly graduated and got a great job as a nurse that allowed her to be off every weekend. She spent those weekends at Young Gutta's grandmother's house. At night they stayed at a hotel, because his granny didn't play that shit up under her roof and you weren't married.

On the way to the hotel this Saturday Young Gutta insisted on driving Kelly's car. It never set well with her that he didn't have his own ride. She accepted it though, and on their way they stopped by a local convenience store. Gutta got out to grab some drinks. This lady pulls up, and she and Gutta get into it pretty bad. Kelly is stunned, she sits there quiet as a mouse so she can hear what they're talking about.

"So this why we ain't fucking - nigga. You got another bitch" She yells at Gutta while trying her best to knock him out. Kelly steps out of the car, because she wants to know what is really going own. She wasn't about to let this woman disrespect her either. Kelly didn't get the chance, because Gutta started cursing her like a dog on a leash. He was about to throw her to the ground, but the police sirens startled him. Someone had called the police.

Kelly and Gutta get back into the car and tried to leave, but old girls car was blocking them in. The police got out and came to the car's driver side.

"Can I see your license?" they asked Gutta. Kelly was in the driver's side now, so they let them both go.

Later that night, the lady from the convenience store boxed her in. "Look I don't know you, but Gutta is dangerous. He is abusive and once he's done with you he'll just drop you."

It's hard to believe anything a woman says about a man when she still wants him. Kelly thought to herself. Little did Kelly know the girl was still kicking it with Gutta. This she would find out later. They would battle for Gutta for over a year. She finally realized Kelly wasn't going anywhere. She left them alone, or she led Kelly to believe so. It was Kelly and Gutta a love of a life time.

Kelly's cousins were over joyed. They were always calling telling her she got here a good man. They knew all the time he was not one to play with. He was thuggish and whorish. They had their own problems, but watching Kelly fall for this thug was all the best for them. It kept them distracted and someone to run in the ground.

Kelly's mother was discouraged and upset with Kelly's choice. She hated that the cousins were back, and even worse this Gutta. "None of them are welcome in this house Kelly, not Gutta or your cousins." Her mom said.

None of Kelly's real friends liked her choices. Jessica and Kim were real friends to Kelly and had never been in the same space with the cousins. Kim was close to Kelly's mom. Kelly even said her mom treated Kim more like her daughter.

Jarvis was Kelly's cousin and he was very protective of her. Once he came into town he tried talking to her. It didn't work. She had fallen hard for Gutta. She got her own place so she wouldn't have to listen to friends and family constantly warn her about her boyfriend.

The twins always wanted to stay with their grandparents and after a few years of hauling them back and forth she let the grandparents keep the kids. She would give them money and visit them every day. She bathed them every night. She loved her kids desperately.

Gutta and Kelly really kicked it hard now that she had her own place. Gutta would get her car whenever he needed it. He was always going back and forth from the hood to their apartment. He didn't bring the hood back to them though. The closest it came was when he went to jail for two years. She never realized what he went to jail for, but she waited for him faithfully for two years.

She never missed a visit down at the jail. Her mom couldn't understand it. Kelly didn't care; she was in love. She started struggling keeping money on his books. He was calling every day and the calls were expensive. She asked him to just call once a day instead of twice. He insisted he had to speak to her twice a day so he would stay out of trouble. She believed him. She loved her some

Gutta.

He loved her too, in fact he asked her to marry him while he was in jail, but kept it a secret. She said yes, and she was too happy about it. He got her named tattooed on him and kept it as a surprise until he got out. He didn't know she had went and done the same thing. They got married and their relationship went to another level.

Gutta started confiding in Kelly. He told her things that disturbed her. She knew that things like this would make anyone lose their blessings. She had just married him, so she wasn't about to walk away from him when he needed her the most.

Because of finances Kelly had moved back with her mom and now that Gutta was out he moved in with his grandma again. Kelly loved Gutta's grandma. Gutta's grandma loved Kelly and kept it real with her. "You go loose your life fooling with my grandson, baby. You're a good girl, and you been raised good. Gutta been in trouble all his life. He been in juvenile hall most of his teenage years."

Gutta's grandma would text Kelly often and always say to make sure she deleted the text. She never mentioned to Gutta she talked with his grandmother.

This particular day Kelly and Gutta's grandma sat out on the porch talking. Gutta walks up and asked Kelly to walk with him. She does, and leaves grandma on the porch. Gutta had started to become very jealous of Kelly since the marriage. This was one of his moments. "You and my cousin got something going own or what?" He started accusing her.

This stunned Kelly, "Hell no! I ain't got nothing going on with your cousin." She snapped before she knew it.

"Girl, who you getting loud with?" he threatened grabbing her by her shirt collar. "You always talking to niggas behind my back. They stay calling your momma house. I love you girl, but I'll kill ya if you cheat on me." He kept ranting and raving about different guys answering the phone at Kelly's mom's house. It was usually a nephew or cousin, and she couldn't control that.

It was darkness in his eyes, a jealous rage. It only started to get worse. One day Grandma heard them arguing and came out to see what was happening. Before she could pull Gutta away, he had hauled off and knocked the hell out of Kelly. She laid there flat on the ground. Grandma called the ambulance and police, but by the time they got there Kelly had come to.

The police asked Kelly what happened. Of course she lied. They took Gutta to jail anyway. In court she lied her ass off. She had to explain the mark she had on her head. She said she received it a week before in a car accident. She really was in an accident a week ago and still had the pictures on the phone. She still had the police report. Needless to say Gutta got out free with no charges. Kelly also had to call his PO so he could be released.

The PO answered the phone thinking Kelly was someone else. He said, "I was just about to call you back Ms. Jean at 555-555-7856."

"No, that's not my name. I'm Kelly and I'm his wife."

"Well I received a call from 555-555-7856, from a Jean for this same reason."

Kelly took down the information. She was going to find out who this woman was. Why was she checking on Gutter. She asked him about it, and he said it was one of his sister's friends. Kelly believed it and let it slide. He apologized for hitting her, and found it hard to believe his grandma called the police on him.

His jealously didn't end. It kept growing. When she went over he would always take her keys and go through her phone. There were even times when he would take money out of her purse. He started her drinking and smoking weed. He was always humiliating her. He'd make her have sex with him in his grandma's bathroom while she was in the Livingroom watching tv. This was so humiliating, because grandma kept asking who's in there. Gutta just put his hand over Kelly's mouth and made her shut up.

Kelly prayed he wouldn't bring that mess to her mom's house, but he did. Once he came to her mom's house about two o'clock in the morning. She snuck him in because if not he would have woken everyone up. He made her have sex with him. She had no idea how he even got there; he didn't have a car. She asked him whose car he was in, but he never would say.

Kelly's mom never found out about that night. From then on Kelly made a point of always being at his grandma's house. That was equally disrespectful, but she just went with the flow. Whenever she tried to defy him he'd says, "Let's take a ride." That was not a good thing. That meant he was going to take her and beat her ass.

He started accusing her of cheating on him at her job. He even brought his ass up there. He was acting crazy and she told him her boss was going to call the police. Kelly started to become very depressed, she wondered often is this real love?

He had started causing conflict between her and her mama. He started calling her mama's house like fifty times a day. Kelly's mother would pick up the phone, hear that it's him and hang up. Sometimes she would answer it and go off on him. She didn't hate him; she just didn't like his ways and prefer for him not to call her house. Gutta didn't respect her wishes.

Kelly mother always told her she knew that she could do better than Gutta. She knew her mom was right but, she never wanted to hear anything her mother had to say when it came to Young Gutta.

Kelly thought Young Gutta was sweet at times. Something just wasn't right about him. Sometimes she wondered was he in special ed in school, because he was slow and hard to understand anything other than the street. He loved her; he just had a strange way of showing it.

This one-day Gutta ask her to come over they really needed to talk. So, she went, and they talked. The conversation started off sweet and romantic. Lord he made love to her two times. He was actually talking with common sense. He caressed and loved on her body like they had just met each other. It was nice. His conversation went from sweet to sour in a blink of the eye. After making love to her the last time he leaned and whispered in her ear he had a baby on the way.

Her mind and her heart were speechless. She felt like somebody was stabbing her in the chest with a knife. She was hurt and mad as hell. Her husband has a baby on the way by another woman. She didn't even have kids by him. She had gotten pregnant earlier in their relationship, but she miscarriage. After all that accusing, he was the one out cheating. I guess the saying is true. The accuser is always the one out doing wrong.

Kelly cried enough tears to fill a river. To put the icing on the cake, he tells her the lady he got pregnant is the one she had previously asked him about. She's the one who got in touch with the P.O officer.

Well damn, not only was she hurt and crying, but now she felt like a fool. She felt like he had his damn clothes down shitting in her face. She cried a river and told him she was done and that it was over. This man hauled off and slapped her in the face so hard she saw stars. He told her that she wasn't leaving him. He said he was in love with her. "I know I fucked up, but I don't care nothing about that girl, I don't love her." He pleaded with Kelly. "I Love you, and a baby isn't going to change the way I feel about you."

He said he hasn't seen her since she called and told him she was pregnant. He made a promise that when he did see her, he was going to beat that baby out of her. Kelly knew he meant it, and she knew what Gutta was planning on doing was wrong.

"Gutta you can't do that. You can't hurt her or that baby, the baby is innocent." Kelly pleaded.

"When I see that bitch, I'm beating the bastard out of her."

He started pulling Kelly close, kissing on her while saying how much he loved her. "Stop Gutta, just stop." Kelly sighed. He ignored her, and he kept doing what he was doing. She didn't want another beating, so she just went alone with the flow. She couldn't make a dash for it, because he had put her keys away. So, she decided to make love to him like her life was on the line.

She had sex with him to exhaust him. He wouldn't go to sleep until she did.

Kelly went to sleep, but she already had a plan in her head not to sleep to hard. She had to get the hell out of there. After a while, she woke up and looked at him to see how hard he was sleeping. He was sleeping pretty hard from the sex and whatever drug he had in his system; he was out of it. She looked at the door then she looked at his pants. She picked those pants up so softly holding them by the pockets so no noise was made. She opened the door and barely closed it, and she hauled ass. She got in her car and sped off.

He didn't notice she was gone until three hours later. That's when he started calling her. He called her too many times, so she finally answered. "Bitch I am going to beat your ass. You left me in this hotel room stranded with no pants. Where's my damn pants?"

"I threw them out on side the road."

"How in the hell am I supposed to leave the hotel room with no pants."

"I don't know Gutta. It's not my problem. I'm done. Stop calling me. Call your baby mama!"

She hung up, but he kept calling. She stopped answering. He took to social media. He was blasting her. Kelly didn't care. "Fuck a Young Gutta." She thought to herself. "This nigga been cheating on me, and got a baby on me, he is beating my ass all the time. I'm not taking my ass back down there."

A month passed by, and he kept calling her cell phone and her mama phone. Kelly's mama told her she wished she would tell that damn boy to stop calling her house. Kelly would block his number, but he would just call from somebody else's phone. He sent a text saying he was about to come down to her house. She felt her heart stop. She didn't reply, so he called. She answered and told him if he comes down there she was going to call the police. He didn't care, and he knew she wasn't going to call the police. She was just trying to scare him. She really didn't want him to come to her mama house at all, because she knew how her mom felt about him.

Kelly went to the back room and pretended to tell her mama that Gutta was trying to come down here. She told Gutta, the police would be waiting. He hung up the phone, and the next day Kelly received a call from his sister.

His sister asked her to just talk to him. She felt like Gutta was really sorry. She said Gutta had broken down like never before. It was a convincing story.

Kelly said she might talk to him. So, the next time he called she did answer the phone and heard him out.

He was talking, apologizing and crying trying to convince her how much she meant to him. They had a long conversation and all while he was talking she was convincing herself that he was telling the truth. She heard the hurt in his voice. Kelly never heard him cry before, that really touched her. He was telling her some very sweet things, but that is what she didn't understand he only talked sweet when he fucked up. She was amazed still at how he expressed his love to her.

Needless to say, she started going back around him. Things went good for a little while. Then the inboxes started coming from Ms. Baby Mama. She in-boxed Kelly telling her she got him. Kelly indulged in it. She told her a baby don't make a man want you. "You got the baby, but I still got the man." Kelly messaged her.

"How do you feel?"

"Feel, what do you mean?"

"How do you feel that I've known about you all this time and you knew nothing about me. I knew about you before I start fucking with him. He told me all about you. He also told me he loves you. I even let him use my car one night to come see you. So how do you feel? That's our man and MY baby daddy."

Kelly was mad as hell at Young Gutta. She called him and told him what the girl said. He told her he was going to inbox her and get her straight. Kelly said, "Ok, but what you go say?" Even if he lied she had his password to his social media. Kelly looked through his messages to read their conversation. He did set her straight, and he also told her when he sees her he going to beat her ass.

Ms. Baby Mama replied back something that shook Kelly hard.

"You won't see me until after I have this baby. You kicked me in my stomach and killed our first baby, but you won't kill this one."

Kelly lost her breath and immediately started crying. Gutta is not the Gutta she wanted to be with. He drives this woman's car, and he got her pregnant before and killed the baby. Tears start rolling down her eyes once again.

Ms. Baby Mama got worse. The girl started meddling posting things on her social media bragging about her and Gutta's baby. Kelly felt like this shit she was going through is real live crazy, but she still stayed. She knew she should have left. She knew Ms. Baby Mama wanted him, so she stayed. She wasn't going to give her the satisfaction.

Young Gutta and Kelly, he was the love of her life. She decided to keep the love alive. His birthday came around, and they were chilling having fun. She got tired, so she asked him to take her back to the hotel. He wanted to keep partying with his boys. They were drinking, popping pills, smoking, and only the Lord knew what else. That's why she wanted to go back to the room. She knew how he gets when he is under the influence. She thought she was safe until he came in at 4 o'clock that morning tweaking out.

"You been laying up with a man while I was gone" He was saying things like she is hiding men in the room and made an accusation that the man was still there. He looked up under the bed, in the bathroom, and he when he got through searching and notice that no one was in the room he forced himself on her.

He made her take off her clothes; he starts sexing her. While they were having sex, he thought that she was talking to another man on the phone. He stops fucking her and started beating the hell out of her. He told her to stay in that one spot and that she had better not move. He started beating her so hard in her face she wanted to fight back, but she knew he had a gun. She had to take it.

He was pounding her face over and over and over, then he started beating and kicking her in the side, back, and stomach. She thought she saw her life flash before her eyes. She thought that was the end of her life. She couldn't breathe or see anything. She was feeling the worst pain of her life. They heard sirens in the parking lot, and that made him stop.

Someone had heard Kelly screaming and called the police. Young Gutta took off running and the cops ran after him. The people in the room next door heard all of the commotion and called the police. The police were chasing Gutta. In the meanwhile, Kelly found strength to get up barely walking, making it to her car and drove off.

6 Pressing Through

The Lord had to have wrapped his hands around her, because there was no way possible she made it home by herself. She couldn't see out of either of her eyes. She was driving very slow running off the road. Her arms, hands, and entire body was hurting so bad. She drove to her favorite cousin's house. She had to let him see what Gutta had just done to her. Her Cousin exploded. He was so mad and hurt he wanted to go kill him.

Kelly wouldn't tell him where Gutta stayed, because she didn't want her cousin hurting someone or end up getting hurt or even ending up in jail because of her situation. He made Kelly call Gutta, and he told Gutta he had just marked his life. "You weak pussy ass nigga I got to see you!" They both talking shit to each other.

Things turned bad quick and Kelly told her cousin just leave it alone; It didn't work, because her cousin knew a few people from Gutta's hood. He started asking them where to find Gutter. He started asking questions about him. Her cousin found out that Gutta had a girl pregnant. Kelly didn't want him to know that, but he found out. He went off on Kelly for dealing with him. Her cousin took a trip to Gutta's hood, but he never had any luck finding him. He went down there for a month looking for Gutta, but Gutta was never in sight.

In the meantime, Kelly called one of

her besties and told her what Gutter had done to her. He sent her a picture. When Kelly's cousin saw the picture, she shed tears; she didn't like seeing Kelly like that. She was mad and pissed. She asked Kelly what her mama had to say. Kelly informed her that she hadn't made it home. She hadn't told her mom about any of it yet. Kelly's bestie told her she was about to call her mama and tell her about what was going on and not to be that hard on Kelly.

Bestie called Kelly's mama. She asked Kelly's mom to distract the twins, so Kelly could come in the house. When Kelly's mama saw her face she just shook her head, and Kelly's father did the same. Kelly knew Her mother's silence meant she was hurting. She was heartbroken that Kelly had to go through that. Kelly knew when her mother went to her room that she was on her knees crying and praying to God for her.

When Kelly's mama was done praying she came out, and she insisted that Kelly go to the emergency room. They went to the emergency room and Kelly was examined. The police came and was asking her questions. Kelly gave them Gutta's name, and told them it happen in another county and that the police there were looking for him.

When Kelly and her mother made it back home from the emergency room, Kelly notices she had left her purse at the hotel room. She called the hotel and they told her they had it in the front office. Her mother drove her down the next morning to get her purse. She asked Kelly was she going to press charges on Young Gutta. Kelly told her yes.

Her mom noticed the look on her face and said, "It's up to you baby." And she decided to leave well enough alone. Kelly's mom said, "You didn't have no business down there with that boy. Just leave him alone, and don't go back down there." Kelly agreed to leave him alone, but she didn't press charges.

Kelly had no other choice but to leave this man alone. He kept calling and calling. "Will he please just leave me alone," Kelly thought. He called one night and said he can't live without her and that he had been getting in trouble ever since she left him alone. She told him she didn't care. His calls and text continue to come for about a week. Then they suddenly stopped. That's when Kelly receive a phone call from a strange number; it was Gutta he was in jail.

He begged her to talk to him that he didn't have nobody. Kelly talked to him and asked him what he had done to be in jail. He told her somebody was shooting at him and his crew, so they had a shootout. She asked why they were being shot at. He told her they thought we were the ones that robbed and killed their homeboy. Kelly was just sick. She felt sorry for him somehow. He started telling her how he was tired of living this way of life. He also apologized again for beating the hell out of her. She went back.

7 Ms Baby Mama

Gutta's little girl was born while he was in jail, but he got out like a year later. He stayed with his daddy for a while, but not long enough. They were too much alike. After he moved out from his daddy's he went and stayed with his aunt. His auntie was a fan of his baby mama. Kelly knew she'd rather see him with his baby mama than her. Kelly didn't like going over her house, but Gutta and his controlling ways made her.

Kelly made sure she didn't mingle with the fake. She always stayed closed up in Gutta's room. The only reason she went back was because she thought he was serious about changing his life. That's why she gave him another chance. She didn't like seeing Young Gutta in jail, so she always made herself available for him. Kelly made sure he understood that if he ever hit her again she was leaving forever. She loved Young Gutta and it wasn't easy walking away from him.

She always felt as if she needed to be there for him. Every time she was with him his baby mama dropped his child off. She even had the audacity to tell him she didn't want Kelly around her child. Kelly started slacking up on going down to see him.

She started to notice she just didn't feel the same about Gutta anymore. Her "give a damn's" were starting to run out. She was never a fan of baby mama drama. Young Gutta hated Kelly having conversations with her twin's father, but it was alright for him to have conversations with his baby mama.

Even though Kelly felt herself pulling away from him she still loved him. Kelly would go over his auntie house to visit him and he still took her car keys and looked through her phone. Kelly had thought he had changed, but this was a sign telling her he hadn't.

Once when she went to visit him at his daddy's house, he took her phone. His daddy told her in front of him "Don't be letting him take your phone." Little did his daddy know Kelly was afraid of his son.

Young Gutta's birthday came back around again and Kelly refused to go around him. She was still scorned about what he did to her on his last birthday. Unfortunately, Gutta didn't agree with her decision. He was mad that she didn't come down there. His birthday was on a Wednesday she wasn't going to go down there until the following weekend.

Young Gutta had given Kelly something to keep for him, and he said that he needed it really bad. Kelly told him she wasn't coming down there and he said he was about to come to her house because he really needed it. She finally gave into him and said she would see him in a little while. She called his sister and asked her was Gutta at her house and she told her no. Kelly let Gutta's sister know that she was on her way to her house to drop his stuff off.

She started talking to Kelly telling her that she didn't need to be taking that shit from him. She knew that Kelly was being abused by her brother and she didn't like it, so she finally told her don't settle for no shit like that. That really meant a lot to Kelly. Not only did his grandma and sister tell her the same thing his mother and his auntie told her. Kelly looked at her situation different after the talk with his family. She finally came to realize that her family wanted her to do better.

It took Kelly an hour to get down there. All while she was on her way down there she was hoping that Gutta wouldn't show up. When she made it to his sister's house, Kelly saw a car pull up behind her; it was Gutta getting dropped off. Kelly start hitting her steering wheel saying damn, damn, damn. He got in her car and told her to go to his auntie house. Kelly didn't have any intention on staying down there, but when he got in the car he took her keys.

As soon as they got out of the car at his aunt's house Gutta said he needed to go to the store. He made Kelly get on the passenger side. Young Gutta was still lit from partying for his birthday. He started in on Kelly time they made it back to his auntie house. He took her up in the room. He started accusing her of cheating.

I am not sure what Gutta had in his system, but he was wildin out hallucinating and shit. He was always seeing people that wasn't there. He was so high he didn't notice he left the keys in the ignition and left the two front windows down. Kelly didn't say a word she was actually glad he forgot them. He continued yelling and cursing at Kelly.

Gutta bragged about he was a big-time drug dealer, and if she was going to fuck him then she might as well make them both some money. He started calling Kelly a "hoe" and the bastard had the nerve to ball up his fist and hit her in the eye. Kelly was tired of taking them licks she took her knee and kneed him in between his legs, and she ran to her car. He started laughing and talking big shit telling her you can't go nowhere

I got your keys.

Kelly got in the car and start rolling them windows up and she left a crack in the driver side window and told him "hahahaha I got my own keys," She started the ignition but the car didn't start. She tried again and turned the ignition again and the car started. Kelly put the car in gear and she burnt tires leaving there. "I am done this time. I WILL NEVER GO BACK. Fuck a Young Gutta" she shouted out to herself.

She made it home and the phone was ringing when she walked in. It was Gutta already calling blowing up the house phone. He didn't get no answer. Kelly was prepared for all the threats and everything else.

She went in her room and started praying and talking to God telling him how tired she was and that she didn't want no more dealings with Gutta. She asked God for forgiveness for all of her wrongdoings. She asked him to wrap his arms around her and keep her safe.

Kelly began crying. She cried and cried thinking about everything this man had put her through and made her do. The things I am about to tell you may seem unrealistic but trust me I wish they weren't. Everything I am about to say is true and embarrassing on Kelly part.

8 Sinking into the Gutter

Kelly took Young Gutta to the emergency room for a toothache. The lobby was full, and the wait was extremely long. He made Kelly go in the ER lobby bathroom and have sex with him. Wait I am not finished. They would be riding down the road, and he would make her get naked and suck his dick while he was driving. There were times when he would pull into a dark spot, lay a blanket down on the ground and make her have sex with him.

Kelly was so scared and embarrassed

that somebody might drive by. The shit that he made her do. One time they were having sex and he told her he could hear her talking to another man. He was always hallucinating. Kelly would ask him how he believed that when he was looking right at her. He would say Kelly had a chip in her ear.

Once they were making love and Kelly tried to make him feel good, so she put both of her legs up, so he could go deeper inside her. "So yo man is telling you how to fuck me," he yelled. He slapped her legs and told her to put them down. This man is real life crazy.

When they were out in public she wasn't allowed to look at anyone. When they were in the car and made a stop she was made to look at the floor in the car. If a man looked at her he would go off on them for looking. Once they pulled up at a corner and noticed one of Gutta's homeboy's was standing on the corner. "You must of let that nigga our the trunk," he accused. The trunk button was on Gutta's side; He was driving the car. Lord this man was driving Kelly crazy.

This shit was real life crazy. He was too controlling, and his abuse was unpredictable. At the rate he was going If Kelly had of stayed he probably would of started pimping her out. Kelly took a lot.

Baby mama drama, abuse, the total disrespect and most of all a waste of time. I guess she wasn't tired enough before, but she was fed up now. That was the past and it's all behind her now. Years wasted that she can never get back. She went through physical, verbally, and emotional abuse due to Young Gutta own insecurities.

Kelly never thought in a million years her life would consist of what she had been through. The best part about it is she made it through and God never gave up on her. Many blessing Kelly missed all because she was his Mrs.

God still had a plan for her. Kelly's mother and her friend never stop praying for her. Kelly knew Young Gutta was no good for her, but she thought she was good for him.

Kelly indeed bought her lesson, and it was a lesson well learned. The life she previously lived wasn't life worth living. Kelly got a divorce and she moved on. She got a better vision she actually made the best decision. Even then she still kept going backwards.

Kelly still had Gutta's password to his social media account. She often logged into it. Once she logged in and saw where he in-boxed this older lady telling her that he was single, so Kelly inboxes the lady off her page and told her that if she knew what she knew she wouldn't have any dealings with him.

Kelly found herself warning another female about Young Gutta. She hoped she listened, but Kelly still remembered when a young lady warned her about Young Gutta and she didn't listen. It's hard to believe anything the ex will say, but sometimes what they are saying is true.

After that he change his password and she was no longer able to log into his page. That was a good thing he change his password. Kelly felt like she did the right thing to warn her before she became a victim of Gutta. Kelly wished she had of listen to the ex that warned her. To find out Gutta was beating the hell out of her too. She got tired of those beatings and cut his ass up.

Gutta had to stay in the hospital for

three days. He continued to talk to her for a couple of months. After that Kelly walked into Young Gutta's life. Lord Kelly just wish she had of listen to the ex. Kelly got hospital bills out her ass running back and forth to the hospital. Her blood pressure stayed up, and she had lost all of her weight. She didn't have an ounce of insurance. The truth is Young Gutta was too Gutta for her.

Once, Kelly had a vision of her own death committed by the bare hands of her husband. She knew what Young Gutta and his crew was capable of, but she wished she had of known before she got involved with him. Kelly was slowly changing into a whole new person but in a negative way. She started talking like him, having an I don't care attitude like him, and she wasn't engaging in the bible like she used to.

She still read the bible every day, but she didn't understand it like she used to.

She had been distracted. She was corrupted in bad energy. She did something that she knew was wrong. Young Gutta was on his way to see Kelly because she wouldn't go down there. Kelly didn't take Gutta serious about being on his way until he called her and told her the car he was in quit on him.

Kelly ask him whose car he was in and he said he was with one of his homeboys. He ask Kelly would she come and pick them up and Kelly said no at first until he kept begging saying he was stranded on the road. She went on and pick them up.

When she got to them she saw he was driving Ms. Baby Mama car. She tried to drive off but the fool jumped in front of her car and got on the hood and wouldn't get off. So Kelly went ahead and took them back home. She was glad he had his homeboy in the car with him. That was one day that Kelly didn't have to worry about getting hit. He wouldn't never hit her in front of people. When she dropped them off he tried to get her to stay. Kelly told him ok she will stay. She cut the car off and everything. When he got out she locked the doors and left. On her way back home, she stopped at Ms. Baby Mama car and took a fuel out and then she called the wrecker company and ask them to tow it to a specific place. The place was two hours away from there hood.

Gutta and Ms. Baby Mama never saw that car again. They assumed Kelly had something to do with the disappearance of the car. They were right but Kelly would never let it touch her. I guess That saying is true "The wrong you do will follow you. Even though Kelly tried to act like her bad luck with cars had nothing to do with the disappearance of that lady car.

Kelly had to accept her wrong doing and asked God for forgiveness so this curse she had could break. Kelly had had three wrecks since she did that to Ms. Baby Mama car. Two of the cars she wrecked got totaled out. The car she drove now was on its last leg.

She was headed to the point of destruction. If Gutta came to her and said "bae let's go rob and kill somebody together for cash." she probably would of done it like a dumb ass. This shit is real life crazy. She loved that man too much and the nerves he had since she had walked away. Messages after messages he kept in boxing her.

Young Gutta had a serious mental problem. One of his messages read: you must be still mad for what you did to me. This man has brutally beaten Kelly, took from her, kept her away from church, force her to have sex with him when she didn't want to, verbally abused her, emotionally abused and hindered her from any good thing that could of possibly come her way. After all the sorry songs he sang to her, he decided he wanted to play the victim.

This man acted as if Kelly was the one doing him wrong. The nerves he had. Oh, well Kelly thought, "he can play the victim if that's what makes him happy but, I know the truth. I was the real victim but, I am free now. It was hard leaving him, It wasn't only that I loved him I felt like I had to be in his life. I thought if I wasn't in his life then he wasn't going to live right. The truth is I was in his life and he still wasn't living right."

Helping him was out of my control. He needed the Lord in his life. Kelly continue to take herself down memory lane. She remembered this man saying things like f*** God. Lord What in the hell did Kelly get herself into. Gutta insecurity was on a war path. That's why he didn't mind hurting anyone. His own insecurity was a life-threatening issue that caused harm to anybody.

9 Crying and Laughing

Kelly didn't hate Young Gutta, but she had to realize that they weren't fit for each other. She wished him nothing but the best in life and prayed that they never crossed each other's path again. Kelly had paid her dues being in love with him. Her family always wanted what was best for her now it was time for her to start wanting the best for herself. She finally got to the point where she could sit down and laugh and cry at the same time about what she had gone through.

Of course, her mother didn't like talking about it all, but her bestie would listen and laugh with her. Her cousin would talk about it, but He would chew her out. Kelly was just a fool in love. Well she was fearful and in love. It's over now and she has started a new chapter in her life. The threats she received were scary. She had to face her fears and brace herself for the threats and leave anyway.

Monica sent Kelly an email saying,

Sis I spoke to mama yesterday and we talked for hours. Mama was telling me about a guy you were dealing with name Young Gutta. I heard about everything. I talks to you like once a week and you never mention to me about what you were going through. I am your sister and you can confide in me and trust me to comfort you, I am deeply hurt hearing about what you are going through. I wish you would have reached out to me and sought my advice. I wish I was there to help you through this. After mama told me about all of this she gave me your friend girl phone number and she verify that it was true. She didn't go into details about what was going on with you, but she did let me know that she was worried about your safety. Mama is really concern for your safety as well. After hearing everything that's going on with you got me concern too. Kelly you are beautiful, and you don't have to cater to no one and prove your loyalty to them. I didn't just hear about Young Gutta but I also heard about the way Asia, Shayla, Kayla and Simone was treating you. Kelly you know I don't indulge in no one business, but you are my sister and I will not stand for you to be manipulated or bullied by your own family. Family can be your worst enemy if you don't watch them. Real family wouldn't betray you nor plan on your down fall.

Some family isn't worth fooling with. Stop trying to please everyone and think about yourself. Mama and daddy love you, your twin loves you and I love you. None of us never ask you to cut your hair or change into a worthless human being. You are too beautiful for that. All honesty you did all of that to please them and when you look at the situation they all was just jealous of you. It isn't that they don't like you they are just jealous of you and have low self-esteem about themselves. Whenever you want to talk to me please don't hesitate to call. Back to Young Gutta sis you deserve so much better than you are receiving.

I know you probably think he loves you but to be honest anyone that physically abuse you doesn't even love themselves. He is calling the house phone stressing mama out. From what I have gather from him he is very disrespectful. He doesn't work and he's abusive. Anyway, I just wanted you to know I Love you so much and I will be praying for you. It won't be long before I come home. I was thinking maybe y'all should have a barbeque in the yard for me and invite your cousins you love so dearly. I want you to invite them, so I can set them straight. I heard you start dressing different because of them. No sis, don't change your standard for nobody. I will see you in a month. Keep your head up and remember to smile because God loves you too!!!

You know we all have that cousin that's down to earth and tends to do whatever the fuck they want to do. Well Kelly had Meka, and she didn't hang around Meka before because Meka liked to smoke and drink all the time. Meka didn't have any children. Kelly and Meka never had a negative run in with each other. It was always nothing but love when they ran into each other. They simply respect each other. Meka had been on Kelly's mind lately.

Kelly had gotten to the point where she didn't feel accepted anymore, so she contacted Meka. Meka was stunned that Kelly called her because they had nothing in common. Meka really didn't want to talk to Kelly because she wasn't an advice giver. Meka had already heard all about Kelly's situation, and even though Meka felt sorry for Kelly, she didn't want to be engage in a sad and heartbreaking conversation that was going to blow her high.

When Meka spoked to Kelly, Kelly asked meka to do her hair. That's how she made her money by doing hair. Meka can do the hell out of some hair, but she smokes weed while she does it. So unprofessional Kelly thought but what can you say Meka was far from professional. She didn't even have her license to do hair. She did it out of her home.

Meka was fine with how she got money if her bills were paid and her habit supplied and her clothes. Meka actually did a lot of people hair. She decided to go ahead and talk to Kelly but she was straight forward with Kelly. "I am not interest in your business you better off talking to God about it." Kelly look at Meka with a stale look. Meka said what, I am just being honest." Kelly said "Yeah, I guess you are." Kelly ask Meka "Do you even have any feelings?" Meka laughed and said "Yes, I do, but this liquor and weed numbs it for me most of the time." Kelly laughed and said "Well can you flat iron my hair for me."

Meka told Kelly "of course it's only twenty-five dollars and I must warn you I am going to smoke my blunt."
"That's fine, the way I feel I might

need to hit that blunt."

"You for real?"

"Hell yeah! I'm going through a real-life situation that got me feeling down."

"Yeah, I heard. When I'm stressing I smoke a blunt or hit the bottle and after that I'm straight. It eases my mind."

"When you lite that blunt let me hit it."

Meka looked at Kelly and burst out laughing and said "I know it's time for me to fire this blunt up because you are tripping."

Kelly said "What's so funny."

Meka reminded Kelly when she use to lite a blunt up in front of her and she would say put that out you going to have me smelling like a stinky bomb. I don't know why you smoke that stuff it's not ladylike.

Kelly said, "Yes, I do remember, and I still don't think it's ladylike."

"Why you want to hit my blunt then since you such a lady."

"Honey I feel so far from being lady

at this point of time in my life, so it wouldn't matter."

"I don't know what you got going on in your life, but girl you need to pick your self-esteem back up."

"Meka I'm not trying to blow your high I just want to hit your blunt."

"Look Kelly let me tell you something Ima let you hit this blunt but don't play with my shit and don't let auntie know you smoked with me."

"Girl I aint' gonna let her find out."

Kelly hit the blunt and started choking because she wasn't a regular weed smoker. She had a little experience with drinking and smoking weed when she was with Young Gutta.

Kelly hit the blunt about four more times and she was high as hell.

"You done hit it enough you can't even stop laughing and it ain't nothing funny." Meka laughed.

Kelly was so high that night that she

couldn't make it home. Meka call her Aunt which is Kelly mother and told her Meka was spending the night at her house. Kelly mother was straight with that because Meka was one of her favorite nieces. The next morning Kelly woke up and went home. Kelly started trying to hang with Meka every night but Meka wasn't feeling that. Meka let Kelly smoke and drink with her a month and after that Meka told Kelly how she really felt. Meka told Kelly "I refuse to let your intake anymore weed and liquor because I know that isn't who you are. Honey we all have problems, but we deal with them and smoking, and drinking isn't going to help you get through what you are going through."

Meka told Kelly that smoking, and drinking was a habit for her and it's something that she enjoys doing.

"Me too, girl," Kelly said without thinking.

"You a damn lie!" Meka laughed,

"this is not your life. Stop settling.

Kelly looked at Meka because Meka words caught Kelly off guard.

Meka kept talking, "I might smoke and drink all the time, but that don't mean I don't know how to love and protect you. You been through hell."

Kelly started crying and Meka grabbed her and gave her a hug and told Kelly that she loved her and that everything was going to be alright.

Kelly spoke up, "I never would have thought that you would care about what was going on in my life."

"We family and I will always be here for you. Don't ever allow someone to make you feel so low about yourself that your whole life falls apart. I've been there done that. God got something better for you. You were always so smart"

"I was pretty intelligent."

"You still are. You just hit a rough spot in the road."

"Meka when we were growing up you was the coolest diva I ever been around."

"Kelly you always made sure, everyone around you felt beautiful."

"I do remember. I really did believe every girl was special and unique in their own way and still think it."

"How in the hell you still think that, when you have lost all the self-esteem you once had in you," Meka said.

Kelly replied in a sad voice, "I don't know. I just don't know."

They were both quiet for a while. Meka broke the silence.

"So how the twins doing?"

"They're good," Kelly smiled, "my two love bugs are the reason I keep pushing. I think they feel my sadness and hurt."

"I am pretty sure they do. That's why you got to get your shit together starting right now. I love you and to show, I will change one thing in my life. I will let you pick that one thing if you promise that you will get your self-esteem back and act like the Kelly before your ratchet cousins and Young Gutta.

Kelly was looking puzzled she couldn't believe what Meka was saying. She accepted the challenge and said, "Meka promise me you will go back to school and get your cosmetology license and don't smoke in front of client."

Meka said, "I agree."

"Really? Just like that you accept."

Meka replied, "Kelly our whole life I witnessed you make sure everyone around you was straight included me. So yes, I accept because I owe that to you and myself. I only want to see you happy and on top. I always admired you as a person, but I never told you.

Kelly felt touched and honored by Meka testimony. "Open enrollment is next month for cosmetology school and I am going to write a check to pay for your first month's tuition."

Meka smiled back, "You've done enough for me, I can pay my own tuition."

Kelly insisted, "I want to pay as part of the deal."

"Paying wasn't part of the deal."

"It's part of the deal now."

"You know how to get a person."

Kelly phone rang, and it was her mother calling asking her what time she was coming home, and Kelly told her she was on her way. Kelly gave Meka a hug and told her that she will talk to her later.

Kelly left and went back home, she cried all the way back home. Kelly ask herself how she could allow someone abuse her and then turn around and abuse herself with weed and alcohol.

She knew that in order to become better and to live better that she had to love herself again. After talking to Meka, she decided to get her life back. Kelly knew she had change. Her children had starting notice that their mother was unhappy and sad all the time and they began questioning Kelly asking her what's wrong with her.

"Fuck it, this has been one hell of a ride that I didn't enjoy it."

When Kelly arrive at home her mother and children was headed to the grocery store. Kelly went on into the house and went into a closet in her room. There she screamed to the top of her lungs. She was so confused and lost.

All she could do was cry out to God "Lord show me a better way!"

She wrote in a book daily about what she wanted to accomplish, and writing in that book actually helped. She would write the exact same thing down until it came to light. Kelly knew then that things was getting better for her.

She realizes the whole time she was going through she was lacking faith in God. After Kelly learned patience with God and regained her trust and faith her life started going in a better direction quickly.

Meka started school and things were looking good for both of them. They called each other every day. They became closer. Kelly told Meka she wanted to introduce her to one of her best friends who was just like a sister to her. The made plans to go out and eat. Kim and Meka connected just like that.

Kelly slowly started to feel loved again.

10 Back to Loving Kelly

Kelly got her self-esteem back and started loving herself again. Kelly was slowly changing back into her old self. She felt more and more comfortable with life every day. She was very excited about new found friendship.

Kim called, "Kelly can I have Meka's number, I want her to do my hair."

Meka told Kim "Yes, I can do your hair you can come on over now if you like."

Kim went on over and Meka started

on her head. As Meka was doing Kim's hair, Kim spoke, "Meka Thank you so much for helping my friend.

Meka said, "It was all my pleasure." She finished Kim's hair. When Kim look in the mirror she was amazed. She gave Meka a tip and said "I will be back for you to do my hair again"

Meka smile and said "Thank You and please come again."

Kim said "You're Welcome, and I will." Kelly loved the fact that Kim and Meka liked each other.

Kelly was doing good, she started getting her hair done by her new stylist Meka and started dressing up and becoming happier. Meka graduated from cosmetology school and got her license to do hair. She rented a building and started doing hair there. Meka stopped smoking in front of her clients and her clientele was increasing. Meka and Kim threw Kelly a party and Jessica came home for the special event. Everyone was happy for Kelly.

That next Saturday after Meka graduated from college Kelly had Kim to help her plan a surprise party for Meka. The funny thing about the surprise was that Meka had also gone to Kim and asked her to help plan a surprise party for Kelly. Meka was left in control of all the planning, so she just planned one big party for both of them.

Kim had it set up amazing. She had one side of the room decorated for Meka and the other side decorated for Kelly. She had fixed up a cake table, and on the cake table there were two cakes. In The center of the ceiling was a banner that read "Congratulation Meka" and "Welcome Back Kelly". Kelly and Meka walk in together and when they saw it they were astonish.

Kelly and Meka had both written down a speech for Kim to read out loud. This night was full of love and surprises. Kelly was very emotional, but her surprises didn't stop there. Monica walk on to the stage and Kelly started smiling from ear to ear. Kelly had no idea that Monica was in town. Monica got on the mic and spoke some loving words to Kelly and Kelly was overwhelmed. She just felted so much love again. That night was lit.

Kelly wrote in her journal

How bless is thee, that God took the time to make you for me after all I been through,

I never once thought I deserve someone like you

a beautiful person, heart filled with love and laughter

you are supported and halcyon the love I once gave to you always seems to suffocate you,

you was always grasping for something more pleasant and true

instead I always founded a way to fail you

I was like an empty shoe box trying to reserve a spot

knowing I was here, there and everywhere

I was living to fast and I was still immature and selfish too

I knew my time would come where as I would finally lose you

Picture a pool full of tears

I cried every night I went without you

I change my ways I change the steps I used to take and the way I use to talk

I knew I had to change in order for God to bless me

So I say, How blessed is thee God gave me another chance with you

The feeling I went through got me promising you, that I will forever be true to you because life without you, Is living life without a clue, How bless is thee God bless you and I to be

His son he gave for me, Thank you God for blessing me with your son Jesus because if it wasn't for him there will be no me

After that night Meka was making money move in her hair business, and Kelly was back on the market and living the life as a diva she once was. Kelly wasn't interest in going back to school but she had found her a good paying job that was easy and up to her speed.

Kelly's children were getting older, so she started focusing on their career. She put the girl in gymnastics and dance. She signs them both up for music lessons. They both learned how to play the piano and her son learned how to play the drums.

Kelly prayed every night to God asking him to protect her children and guide them in the right way. Kelly didn't want her children to go through what she had been through. Kelly promised herself to be the best mother she could be. Kelly started worshiping the Lord on every Sunday. She made sure she and her children was there faithfully. She joined the choir, and one Sunday she led a song at church. Kelly's vocals were amazing, but she hid it from everyone. Kelly mother knew Kelly could sing when she was younger, but also knew that Kelly didn't like to sing so she never pressures her.

Kelly hadn't sang since she was sixteen, so when her mom heard her sing in church she was amazed and touched. She started crying with the biggest smile on her face. She knew at that moment that her baby was happy with life again.

11 What Next

Kelly had found herself. Her burdens weren't wearing and tearing her down. She found herself singing laying my burden down by Jennifer Hudson on a regular basis. When she sang that song, you could literally hear hurt in the tone of her voice and tears rolling down her face.

One day Asia decided to go visit Kelly. Asia knew that Kelly was upset at her and the other girls, but she had to go visit her because she had been on her mind lately. Asia stood outside the door bracing herself before she went in. Suddenly, she hears a voice singing. It was Kelly singing that song "laying my burdens down" so Asia decided not to go in, so she just stood by the door listening to Kelly sing. Kelly sung that song Asia started crying and she started singing with Kelly.

Kelly noticed while she was singing another voice, so she followed the voice to her front door. It was Asia singing and crying. Kelly was stunned she didn't know why Asia was even there or why she was crying. Kelly grabbed Asia and they started hugging each other as they both kept singing. They were both an emotional wreck. They went on in the house and sat on the couch in the living room. Asia started apologizing to Kelly about how she treated her.

Asia poured her heart out to Kelly. She said how she hated that she was abused and mistreated by Young Gutta. Kelly express to Asia that it was fine and that it's over now. Asia said, "It might be over now, but I want to help you get through it.”

Kelly looked perplexed, “How can you help overcome something you never experienced.”

Asia bald her lips and closed her eyes. She put her hand over her forehead and took a deep breath. Kelly understood. Asia had been abused herself.

Kelly teared up saying, “Being abused is something I wouldn’t wish on my worst enemy. I really felt like you all were enjoying how I was being treated.”

Asia said, “That's where you always went wrong at. Assuming some dumb shit like that.” Asia stood up looking at Kelly and asked her, “Do you really want to know the truth?”

“Yeah, I loved ya’ll and rocked with

ya'll but didn't get that treatment back."

Asia responded, "You right you always were good to us, and for that I apologize. Kelly I am sorry for the way I treated you. Will you please forgive me.
Kelly replied, "I already forgave you."
"Thank you, you don't know how much that means to me."

Asia starts to open up about her abuse. "I was once in your shoes, Kelly."

Kelly look up kind if already having an idea of what she was about to say.

Asia said, "Yea little old happy Asia wasn't happy at all. Do you remember Erick?"

"Yea, he was cool."

"Uhm that's what you think," Asia

said, "that man beat my ass twice a week. I never knew why. All I knew is that he would come home in a rage and start attacking me. He used to get mad whenever I would go over my mama house to visited or if I go up town."

Asia went on to say, "I can be out with him and if a man looks at me he would slap the shit out of me when we got from around everyone. I couldn't use my phone around him, because he thought I was talking to men. He had started taking my phone with him when I left the house.

When I went somewhere he would play it off like he didn't have a problem with it. He would leave and when he came back in he would tear my ass up. I would try to fight back, but his strength was beyond mine.

Kelly cried, "I didn't know Asia."

Asia said, "I know, I made sure nobody knew. Why you think I wore all that damn makeup."

"I thought you was trying to look pretty?"

"Honey it was to cover them black eyes and bruises I was getting."

Kelly said, "I am so sorry."

"Kelly, this man would unscrew the lugs off my tires."

"No, girl you lying."

"Honey one day I was riding down the road and my tire started riding different. I pulled over at a store that I was close by, and this man came over and ask me if I needed help. I said "Yes, something wrong with my tire." The man checked and he told me somebody had loosen two of my bolts off my tire."

Asia never did ask Erick about it, but she knew that she had to be extra careful. She started checking everything before she used it. "You know how my eyes always use to be irritated when we were younger. I found out I have dry eyes. So I had to start using eye drops."

Kelly said, "Don't tell me this man messed with your eye drops."

"Yes, he did. Honey he put some alcohol in my drops."

"Did you put it in your eyes?"

"Nope I told you I started checking everything before I used it."

"Lord girl he was crazy."
"I know," Asia said, "I tried my best to hide everything from my mama, but girl one day she pops up over there and I ran to the bathroom to make my face up and my makeup was gone. I told her

I felt sick and I was going to call her later, but she wouldn't leave. Kelly I was hiding in the bathroom and she kept yelling, "hurry your ass out the bathroom I got to use it." I told her to go to the other bathroom and she said that the door was locked.

I had to come out. You know my mother got a weak bladder. When I came out that bathroom my mama seen my face and she started going off. She packs Erick clothes herself and she call both of my brothers over there. Asia was telling Kelly they stayed over there until Erick came home and they tore his ass up. Asia said I never wanted to put no one in my business, but I had been going through this abuse for a year before my mama found out."

Kelly ask, "Were you mad that they beat him up?"

"Nawl," Asia, said, "I been wanting

a way out, but I never could get out. My mama stayed with me for six months to make sure Erick wouldn't try nothing stupid. That was a relief and a burden lifted up off of me."

Asia told Kelly that's why she broke down when she was singing that song. I just went through what you just came out of. I was too ashamed to tell anyone, and I was too afraid to leave him.

Kelly said, "I know exactly what you mean."

"If there's anything I can do for you please let me know. I am here for you."

"When I heard you were going through the things you were going through I wanted to come and talk to you, but I never could build the courage to tell my story so instead I prayed for you every night. I must admit I was always a tad bit jealous of you. I don't know why, but that is why I always acted the way I acted toward you."

Asia told Kelly, "You always was the smart one and made good decisions while I had the I don't care attitude's. All while we were growing up I always envied that you had both of your parents in the house with you. My mother had to take care of me and my brothers by herself. We watched her struggle trying to make ends meet. The truth is Kelly I always wanted your lifestyle and that's why I stayed at you.

Asia continued, "When I was going through that abuse I thought about everything I ever had went through and ask God for forgiveness and now I am asking you to forgive me. Asia said what I did to you was wrong and you didn't deserve it."

Kelly said, "Honey I had already

forgiven you."

"Can we ever be like we once were because I really miss you?"

"Yes, we can because I also miss you but don't cross me like that again." They hugged and everything was good. Asia left and went home.

After Asia left Kelly started singing that song again. "Lay my Burden Down" This time when Asia sang the song she sang it with a smile on her face. She felt pressure lifting up off of her. The phone rang, and it was Monica, Kelly answered the phone very cheerful and her sister said to her, "You sound happy."

"I am. I got your email. It really touched my heart."

Monica said, "That's good, I love you."

Kelly start telling Monica that she just had a conversation with Asia. Monica said "Are serious Kelly that girl doesn't mean you any good!"

Kelly said "Well we both just had a long heart to heart conversation and she explained everything to me and she apologize.

"See you too easy on people."

"Asia really broke down and poured her heart out."

Monica said, "What did she tell you?"

"She told me why she was jealous of me, and how she also gone through abuse. She told everything, and I cried for her. Don't breathe one word of what I am telling you to nobody."

"I promise, but still have your guards

up with her."

"I understand, I talked to mama about it and she told me the same thing. Kelly told Monica I am happy and free now."

"Thank God"

Kelly said, "Well sis let me call you back later."

"Okay."

12 A New Life

Kelly has found a new lease on life. Once she moved on from her Young Gutta. She started seeing life in a better way. Kelly stayed single for a year after her divorce. She met a man name Nelson but, she is taking it slow.

They are friends with benefits, but nothing further at the moment. Kelly really likes Nelson but She's not trying to rush anything. They have been friends for eight months now. They have a lot in common. Their birthday is two days apart. He enjoys going to church and he comes to all her family engagements. Not to forget to mention her mother loves him. He comes over and checks on her even if Kelly isn't there. Nelson likes to barbeque he actually thinks he's a beast on the grill. Sometimes he will come over and grill for them.

He respects Kelly on every level. He treats her like a queen. He always buying her children something, and they enjoy his company. Nelson takes Kelly out to eat, he took her on trips out of town and he helped with her bills. Nelson invited her to his church. He even introduced her to his family and his pastor. Nelson really likes her.

Kevin doesn't have any children. He doesn't drink, smoke or pop pills. He's a manager at a bank. He calls and checks in on her every day. He evens sends flowers to her job. Kelly isn't used to any of this. She finds herself crying but her tears are of joy. She has a hard time believing that someone like Nelson has stepped into her life.

After a year of being just friends Kelly gave in and they start planning a wedding. He was so happy his smile was a representation of pure love. Kelly never thought she could be loved again. She thought she couldn't trust anyone enough to love again.

Nelson already had a brick house with four bedrooms in it. His house was empty, but he was the type of man that lived by God's word. No shacking up. As they made way to get married he told her all she had to do was show up and he will handle the rest if that's fine with her.

She wasn't used to a man asking her for her decision, so that really touch her heart. She told him she wanted to help plan the wedding since it will be a very first wedding. He told her the ball was in her court and she can do whatever makes her happy. She never will let him see her cry, but when he's wasn't around she fell to her knees and cried to the Lord. She was so Thankful of everything that he was doing in her life.

The day before the wedding he knew she wasn't going to be at home, so he asks her mother to pack all her and her kids' belongings up and he came to pick them up. He took the belonging to his house and properly put them away.

The day of the wedding she was so beautiful and happy. He surprised her with a poem he wrote just for her. As he began reading the tears began falling she was extremely happy and in love. The wedding was beautiful, and the atmosphere was covered in love.

His mother gave her the biggest hug and whisper in her ear. "Baby you got you good man and I know you are a good woman." She told Kelly it was a blessing to gain her as her daughter-in-law. Nelson mother told the twins, "Y'all can call me granny or grandma if you like." Kelly felt like she had hit the jackpot. She had gone from shit to sugar and she was very amazed. After the wedding they went on their honeymoon.

They went to Harbor Island, Bahamas for 4 days. Kelly never in her life went to a place so beautiful and romantic. She was extremely happy. After their time was up in the Bahamas they made their way back home. They had a conversation and he let Kelly know that it was time for her to move in with him. She put the biggest smile on her face. He looked over and seen her smile and he grabbed her hand and kiss it. Kelly continue smiling and started looking out the window.

Once they made it back to Mississippi he stops at her mother's house, so they can pick up the twins.

When they got there Kelly told her mother that she was moving in with Kevin. Her mother just smiles, because she had already known.

She went to her room to pack her clothes and realize all her and her children belonging were gone. She went on the living room were her mother and Nelson was sitting and ask her mother where her belongings were. Her mother just looked and smile again.

Nelson stood up and said, "I asked your mother the day before the wedding to pack everything up and I came and got it. He stood there with a key in his hand, and he said to her you no longer live here, you and your children have a home with me."

Kelly smile appeared again as she grabs him and hug him tight as she could. She told him right in front of her mother, "Baby I love you so much."

He said, "I know that's why I love you even more."

Her mother had cooked a big dinner and assist that they sit down and eat before they left. After they was done eating Kelly, her twins and her husband left and went home. When they got there and walked in the house Kelly was amazed at how the place was decorated. It was something that she would of done herself.

The twins walk around the house until they found their room. They never had a room by themselves before. They went in the room and found that their room was decorated in their favorite character. They ran to their mother and told her "Mama come and look at our room!" She went and when she saw it she was surprise and happy. She went on to master bedroom which was their room and she fell in love with the room it was amazing. After they got settle in and the kids went to bed Kelly thanked Nelson for being the person he was to her and the kids. She asked him how you knew what the kids wanted their room to be.

He replied, "I had your mama to ask them for me and your sister gave me ideas of what you would like."

Kelly immediately smiled and said, "I remember when we would go shopping we would have conversations about how I would decorate my house." She looks at Nelson surprisingly and said, "You had her asking me all alone." He just smiled and said, "I love you."

A year later Kelly got pregnant. Nelson was so excited that he was going to have his first biological child. He always treated the twins like they were his and he took care of them like they were his. So, Kelly knew he was going to be an awesome father. Nelson made sure he went to every Dr. Appointment with Kelly. And at the gender reveal party he didn't care what the sex of the baby was as long the baby was healthy.

The gender was reveal and it was a boy. That was his mother first grandchild. His mother stood up and gave a speech about how she was so happy. She said "I am so glad to be here to share this moment. Even though this is my first biological grandchild I have a total of three grandchildren."

Things couldn't go any better for Kelly. They had an extra room in the house and they turned it into the baby room.

Kelly never told Nelson about the abuse she went through with Young Gutta, until five years later. He asks her why you never told him earlier. She replied, "It's too hurtful to talk about."

She cried as she was telling him about what she went through and he cried with her. He told her he was sorry she had to ever go through something like that. He told her his mother always talked to him about how to treat a woman and that he wouldn't never do anything like that to her.

After Kelly told Nelson about her abuse he started loving her even harder. They went to church every Sunday. Kelly's mama insisted that they have Sunday's dinner if they were available at her house every Sunday. Kelly had a better idea. She mentions it to her husband first. She thought it would be a good idea to have Sunday dinner at their home and both of their mothers prepare the food. Everyone agreed.

Kevin was the best thing that happen to Kelly, but Nelson also knew that Kelly was the best thing that happen in his life too. They lived happily ever after with their three children. Kelly found love, that was safe, pure and nonviolent. After Kelly broke down and express to her husband about her abuse she felt like she was free of all things.

Asia and Kelly had regained their relationship and Kelly mother finally forgave Asia for her actions toward her Kelly. She would even come to some of Kelly's family Sunday dinners. At one of the dinners Asia brought to Kelly's attention an outreach program for physical abuse, verbal abuse and mental abuse. Kelly and her husband thought it was a great idea.

Kelly told Asia, "Yes let's do it." Kelly and Asia thought if they could help anyone that was going through or even coming out of some sort of abuse that they could be a motivation to them.

Asia was like, "Yes; the program can

be designing to help people learn to notice signs of abuse. To teach them how love and respect themselves."

Kelly mother ask both of the girls are they ready to tell the world their life stories. Asia replied saying, "At first, I didn't want to share with the world about anything that I went through because I was ashamed and felt hopeless, but now I am ready to stand before the world and let them hear my story if it will help and benefit someone. I want it to keep them from going through what I went through.

When I was going through all I saw was darkness because I was afraid of how the world would see me. I refused to have a support system to help me and I decided to face my problems on my own. It took me years to deal with it and to be honest I just learned how to deal with it when I linked up with Kelly and we talked about what we went through and vowed to help each other out of that dark place we were in. So yes, I am ready to tell my stories."

I know I was able to help Kelly and Kelly was able to help me. That's when I knew we would be a great team of helping others. Kelly husband looked at Kelly and Asia and said, "I am so sorry that both of you had to experience that lifestyle, but I am here for whatever y'all need me to do."

Kelly kissed Nelson and told him Thanks. Nelson's Mother said, "Looks like y'all two young ladies have some work to do." Nelson mother look at Kelly and said, "I never knew you was abused and my heart goes out to you and Asia. Y'all have my support."

They both said Thanks. Kelly and Asia gave each other a week to pitch their own idea on paper and then they linked back up and reviewed it with each other. They started their process after they did a vision. Kelly and Asia promise each other their best effort no matter how hard it gets. They started in a small building right beside her cousin Meka's Salon.

The name of their slogan for their business was "Freedom For All". Kelly and Asia passed out flyers at different churches, stores, social media, Doctor office and Meka's Salon.

Kelly also went inside some the public service offices and let them know what they were doing. Kelly and Asia did this movement for free. They knew a lot people probably couldn't afford it and they refuse to let money to be an issue to hinder them in helping other people. They had motivational speakers come and speak to the crowd. Kelly and Asia would be the speaker in sharing their stories to the crowd and gave opportunities to the crowd to speak if they wanted too.

Kelly and Asia knew that some, if not most of the people would be ashamed so they held a one on one session to help victims of abuse. It was this young lady that wasn't a shame nor afraid to discuss how she was abused. She stood up and stated her name, Alice.

Alice begin telling everyone what she had been through. She stood up there brave as a lion with smile that couldn't be taken away. Alice begin telling how she had married a man that she was deeply in love with. She loved his child like it was her own flesh. Alice doesn't have any children, but she accepted her husband daughter as it was their daughter. Alice and her husband were married for a year and after that they moved 14 hours away from home because he was offering a job with better pay and benefits.

Things was going fine for Alice and her husband for the first six months until he started acting different. Taking trips back home without her, stop sleeping in the bed with her and always catching attitudes with her for no reason at all.

Alice reveal her deepest hurt to everyone that her husband had brought her fourteen hours away from home to ask for a divorce within the first nine months they were up there. Alice kept pouring out her story telling everyone that after her husband ask for the divorce he took a trip back home and brought the mother of his child back with him.

Alice continued standing with a smile and told everyone how she felt when he did that. Alice said it took everything in me not to shoot that husband of mine. He disrespected me, hurt me and abandon me. My own husband acted as if I didn't even exist. I cried and cried and cried. My mother told me to just pack my things and come on back home. I told her I was, but I am going to stay up there six more months, so I can be financially stable when I come back home. I gave him the divorce with no hassle.

He bought the mother of his child a car and everything. I moved back home and within the two months of me being back home my ex-husband had moved back home too. He started calling me expressing how sorry he was for hurting me the way he did. This man wanted me back, marriage and all. I told him it's funny the same person you mistreated you now begging for her back. I told him No. He told me I could have the car that he bought her. Let me remind you I loved this man more than I loved myself and I was seriously thinking about taking him back. Even though he left me for the mother of his child which the mother of his child turned around and left him.

We started talking and going out again, but it didn't last but a month because I was very uncomfortable remembering how he once did me. I had a talk with him and told him I forgive him for the way he had treated me. I didn't wish any bad upon him, but I can't and won't go back down this road. I told him we can be friends, strictly and that's it, nothing more.

He accepted the friendship but every chance he gets till this day he reminds me how much he misses me. I told him, I know you miss me because I miss me too. All these years I been settling for less and that's not me.

Alice proceeded to tell everyone that she's only smiling now because she has come to reality and accepted her past and put it behind her. Alice told everyone it wasn't easy, but I dealt with this feeling for two whole years trying to find myself.

Prayer and faith held me up every day of my life. I wasn't never ashamed to speak on how I was hurt. Actually, I spoke on it with a lot of people when I was going through it. Alice let everyone knew it's alright to hurt, it's alright to be a shame but don't let what you been through be a hinder to you. I wasn't physically abuse, but I was most definitely emotional abuse. Abuse is abuse and every individual got to protect themselves for it.

Alice story really touched a lot of people they were crying, and a lot of people started sharing their abuse with others. It was this one lady name Tara she was shy, but she stood up and spoke.

"I was physically, emotionally and

verbally abuse by serval of men that came into my life. I felt like I was cursed because the same thing kept happening to me but with different men. One of the men I used to talk to would get drunk and started beating on me.

I had two men decided to use the trunk and the hood of my car as a seat while I was driving down the road. My child has seen a man hit me and that hurt me more than anything. Hope stood up After that start saying I used to laugh at everything I went through, I guess I never took myself seriously or that was just a way I reacted instead of been depressing and stressing myself out.

When I was in high school I was talking to one my classmate we were actually going together having sex and everything. I graduated for high school but he dropped out in our eleventh grade year. My mama didn't like him at all, well to be honest she never agreed with me having a boyfriend, so I used to lie and say I'm gay. My mother wouldn't believe it though she knew I was lying and that I was trying to distract her for speaking on my boyfriend. She had already told me that she didn't care for that boy and demanded I stop talking to him.

I acted like I stopped talking to him but I was still talking to him so after I graduate I was already eighteen years old and me and him got a house and move in together. I know I hurt my mama but act the time I didn't care. I got the boy name tattoo on me and everything. When we started living together I notice that he was controlling and crazy. He always accused me of cheating and then he would jump on me.

I got tired of that mess, so I ask my cousin to ride down there with me, so I can get my clothes and she did. I knew he wasn't at home because I knew his work schedule at least that's what I thought. He came while we were in the back packing my stuff. He asks my cousin to give us some privacy, so we can talk.

My cousin went in the living room. He took my phone and pinned me to the bed with his hand over my mouth, so I couldn't scream. I bit his hand and he slap me and started choking me my cousin heard the lick when he slaps me, and she barge in the room and grab him. After I was losing I grab my phone and me and my cousin ran to the car and left. After that my cousin told my mama what had happen and she was mad and said she should listen to me and she wouldn't be in this mess. I then called my granddaddy to take me over there to get my clothes and he took me. My Grandpa is like my best friend.

I went and had the tattoo with his

name covered with a flower. I left and didn't look back. Just my luck Tara said I met the father of my child and he was just the crazy as my high school boy friend. We would be driving down the road and he would decide to reach across and hit me. and take my money and everything. I left him too, the men were too crazy for me. Tara told everyone if you are dealing with any kind of abuse then get out now.

After Alice, Tara and Alice shared their stories people started standing up one by one telling their stories. Kelly and Asia knew then that the movement that they formed was worth it. Kelly and Asia both got to speak some encouraging words before closing for the night. Right when they grab the mic Kayla walk up to Kelly and Asia where they stood, and she patted Asia on the back and look at Kelly and smile as she grabs the mic.

Kayla begin by apologizing to Kelly

for how she treated her. Kelly immediately responded letting Kayla know everything is alright. Kayla then said to Kelly NO it's not alright. I treated you bad because of how I was been treated. Kayla said the real reason my husband and I got a divorce is because one night we were having a conversation and he throw me down and choked me until I couldn't breathe. I thought I was dead when he let me go I ran and lock myself in the room and call my mother crying asking her to help me. I told him to leave and if he didn't I was going to call the police.

He left, I didn't talk to him for a week he kept calling but I wouldn't answer he sent me about thirty text messages saying how sorry he was for choking me and that it was my fault. I knew I played a part of putting fuels to the fire, but he always told me he wouldn't never hit me.

After that day he choked me I was

pulling away slowly. He was my financial support because I wasn't used to working, all I knew how to do is stay at home and take care of our five children. My husband took care of everything, I guess you can say I had it made financially but I wasn't 100% happy. I was going to make it work for the sake of our children, but I was at the point that I feared him. As much as I loved him I had to let it go because I felt as in if he hit me once then he would hit me again. Kelly that's the real reason I got a divorce and I envy you because I felt like you had it made. It wasn't right.

I love you and I hope you can forgive me. Kelly and Asia but was shedding tears and when Kayla got through talking they ask her why you didn't talk to us. Kayla responded and said I guess I was just like the rest of you all... ashamed. Kelly said we in it together and I got you Kayla gave Kelly a hug and told her Thank you. While

Kelly and Kayla were having their moment Asia sarcastic ask Simone what's your story. Simone Laugh and said I am going to keep it simple. The father of my child taught me how to fight. Simone said me and that man use to fight like cats and dogs, until I got tired and left his ass.

Asia was stunned that her friends had been abuse too. Asia was really speechless at the moment, so she closed the show by Thanking everyone for coming out and ask them to join in with a prayer. "Freedom for all" is a great success for many. They were open four days out seven to help people. Kelly and Asia were rarely out of any of their own money because they held fundraiser to help cover the cost and they also created a go fund me account. Some of the people that attended the program that was able to give gave and it was a blessing for Kelly and Asia to help others.

Kelly and Asia have extended their help to young teenagers and children. They help drug addicted people and all. Freedom for all serves everyone that need help no matter what they needed help with. Kelly and Asia family were disturbing to hear all of what they went through, but they were happy that others could benefit from Kelly and Asia abuse.

The business was growing in population, so they had to relocate to a bigger building. Life was good for Kelly and Asia and they felt good seeing people come in broken but when they left they was wearing a smile in knowing that there was hope. It takes a strong person to stand before the world and tell their story that cause them shame just to help others. We need more people like Kelly and Asia in today's society. Remember help is help and it's a blessing to help the ones who needs help. Kelly and Asia helped these people without judgment and they made them feel safe again. "Freedom for all" open up a lot of eyes for people self-worth.

13 Finally Free

FINALLY FREE

Sometimes I feel like a worthless human being
at times I feel like giving up
I feel like this just might be the end
If somebody was to ask me why
I probably will lie and cover it up
but the truth is, I'm tired of getting beat up
man look what you have did to me
I'm out here in this world like how this can be
but one day, I'm going to find the courage to walk a
way
and when I walk away, I am going to face the world
and tell them how I had to live day to day
Bruises and swell is what I took from you
after you'll beat me, you would say, baby you know I
love you
I was left with no choice, but to say I love you too!
that was how afraid I was of you
I knew I was grown
but I was more like a child

I look at you crying, wanted to asked you why
why you doing this to me
I felt like dying
tears rolling, nose running, my heart is broken
I just didn't understand, the pain he was releasing
from his hands
he was hitting me like I was a man
I wanted to leave
but I was too afraid
I thought if he founded he would go into rage
so I prayed and prayed
and one day God bless me with the courage to walk
away
after all I went through
I asked myself why
why did I stay
why did I let him treat me this way
I love this man and I thought he would change
I had faith that one day, all of his violent ways would
go away
but as you see, he didn't change
that's why I walk away
I look back at an image of me
thinking of how he terrorize me
this man was going to be the death of me
but now I am finally free
I manage to banish my own fears
this was a blessing that God gave to me
why is this so hard for me to believe
that I am free
yes I am free, I AM FREE, I AM FINALLY
FREE

Self-Worth

Does anyone care about self-worth these days?
Women going through things that they don't even
have to tolerate
Like what is love? when it's fake
Fuck love! when you take it to another case
people consider heart break like history
when they really don't even know, what real history is
History is what paid the way
not to regenerate what women had to put up with
back in the days
I love all my sisters of every shade
but sometimes we need to sit down and concentrate
on our future and what's at stake
His infidelity already done showed his true ways
so let's not manipulate our own fate
Of course he's going to accommodate
He likes to masturbate
but instead you need to teach him how to appreciate
You need to let him know what he's doing is not okay
But this is universal
To my brothers I'm not here to downgrade you
But she doesn't deserve the hurt
but if she knows what's on demand and still be like
fuck it, that's my man
Then she applauds the hurt
She's living life for what he is worth
and that sad to say
women in this world trading in their self-worth
I don't say shame on you
because that's the path she chooses
You got to look at it
yeah, he wrong

but she's a grown woman too
He treats her on how she presents her worth
what is it? Is it your weight, your facial appearance?
find your dignity and all this will disappear
See, she loves him more then she loves herself
He will hurt her numerous of times
but hurting him never comes to her mind
That's the type of woman that will love you to the
end of times
but she needs to flat rate his love because he's not
worth a dime
He's actually nothing but a waste of time
but when it's all set and done
she still going to be hollering that's her man with
every excuse she holds in the palm of her hand

14 Questions to Ask Yourself

1. Why does a man beats a woman?
2. Why does a man cheats all the time?
3. Why does a man thinks all women are not trustworthy?
4. Why does men don't like to work?
5. Why men lie about being in love?
6. Why does a man beat a woman?

He might a seen his mother or some women been physical abuse before. After he witness it with his own eyes he probably thinks it okay to hit a woman.

He might just have an anger issue and don't know how to control it. He might just be controlling himself and doesn't see any wrong in hitting a woman. He probably never fought a man before in his life. He is a coward, fighting a woman that he knows that his man power will overdue hers.

Under no circumstance should a man put their hands on a woman to harm her in a physical way. By no means necessary should a woman accept physical abuse. If you are in a relationship and you are been abuse I advise you to get out now. It's not worth it. If he is hitting on you occasionally leave his ass permanently. You were not brought into this world to be a man punching bag, End of discussion.

Why does a man cheat all the time? Well that's hard for me to answer. The best answers I can come up with is, He's a man. He is doing it because he knows you still going to stand by him. In other words, you allow him to cheat on you so he going to cheat. Maybe he isn't ready to settle down and needs to be single to get all of them whorish ways out. This all I got for this question.

Why does a man think all women are not trustworthy? Well let me start by saying, it started when he was younger at home with his parents or he have got his heart broken before. Sometimes men grow up in the house with their mother, sister, grandma, aunt, or cousin. What I am trying to say is they have seen how women operates. They have been exposed to the game at a younger age. They probably have seen their mother cheat on their daddy or whoever she was with. They probably have road with a woman while she was doing her dirty work. To sum it up they have witness how women lie, cheat and have somebody cover up for them. That is why some men feel the way they feel about women. Like I said he might have got his heart broke by woman.

Why doesn't men like to work? They are sorry as hell if you ask me. Some probably was brought up and seen that they daddy didn't work. When children are young for some reason they want to be just like their parents. That's why parents it's a must that you be a better role model for your child. Some men just use a woman for their money and make ends meet just like that. Some women just spoil these grown ass men and let them know that it's alright not to work.

Why does men lie about being in love? They scared of been hurt. Done been hurt before. Have seen their parents been heartbroken.

15 A Prayer for Women

Instead of me asking questions about women, I'll rather address some of the issue regarding women. I am woman but I Thank God for lacking some of the quality's women have. Trust me I am about lifting up my sisters rather biological or just woman in the street, friend or a woman in general. I need the women to start being a mother to their child(ren) and not their friends.

Teach your child about the moral concept of life. Teach them how to love and respect themselves so that they will be able to love others. Women stop having these kids and neglecting them. They didn't ask to be here. A child gives their mother the highest praise only if they could get it in return. Teach them about Personal hygiene and teach them the ins and outs about life. Prepare them for the world where so they will not be blindsided.

A Prayer for all mother: Father, O Father I come to you with a heavy loving heart asking you to guide me and show me the way, Father please give me the wisdom and knowledge whereas I can be the best mother I can be, Lord lift me up where I fall Short and struggle with my parent duty in Jesus name I Pray Amen Women please start Loving, respecting and cherishing yourself including your whole body.

To every woman please learn your self-worth. Stop settling for anything. Including being a side chick, getting beat, being mistreated, disrespected and allowing anyone to belittle you as a person.

Women apply yourself to be all you can be. Stop looking for handouts. Always remember anything worth having is worth working for it.

Women stop being petty with other women. Sis just because you mad at her or don't like her you decide to go sleep with her man. Lol at end you are the one that added an extra mile on your how many men I done sex list. So not worth it.

Women stay getting mad at other women simply on some jealous type shit. What you jealous for go out and make something of yourself. Stop focusing on other and worried about yourself see how things start turning around for the good in your life.

Women as of today we are strong Godly sister no matter the what the color of our skin is let's stay strong and support each instead of tearing each other down.